How to Catch a Turkey

sourcebooks
jabberwocky

From the New York Times Bestselling Team
Adam Wallace & Andy Elkerton

Here we are on **THANKSGIVING DAY**,
It's that special time of year.
Yes, I know, I am a turkey,
that much should be clear.

So gather 'round, I have a tale,
and it's really quite a story–
What I tell you now is not a joke,
it is my crowning glory.

It all began one year ago,
I was at a **School**, you see.
Play preparations were underway,
but that didn't matter to me.

Some kids walked by in silly clothes,
talking about the play.

"We'll even have a turkey on stage!
It's perfect for Thanksgiving Day!"

PLYMOUTH ROCK

Turkey? Stage? No way! No how!

Had I *really* heard that right?

I broke out of my pen and ran away

with a case of bad STAGE FRIGHT!

I burst into the science room,
knocked over flasks and beakers,

and the cry of, **"Catch that turkey!"** boomed over the loudspeakers.

So now more children joined the chase with catapults and food.

But their **goopy** mashed potatoes weren't enough to keep me glued!

Up next, there was a **MAZE** of books
that stretched from wall to wall.
But with a big hop and a mighty flap,
I managed to escape it all!

I ducked past chairs and bags and desks—
now that was quite the trick!
The kids thought they could stop me here,
but I was much too *QUICK!*

I ran outside to the **jungle gym**,
thinking I could hide.
But the recess yard was all tricked out—
I'd have better luck inside!

Finally the kids gave up
but the **principal** gave chase.
My only hope of escaping her
was keeping up my pace!

I slid into the coach's room,
and crashed into a chair.
I got TANGLED up in jerseys
but I won't get stuck in there!

I ran into a curtain—
there was nowhere else to go!
I couldn't get past the principal,
but the curtain led to the **SHOW**.

My heart was racing, I started to sweat,
I couldn't **SQUAWK** or run...

I took a deep breath. *I can do this!*
Who knows? This might be **FUN**.

A kid stood up and pointed,
"Oh my gosh! He's so **cute!**"
"He really is," a parent agreed,
"in his little mascot suit!"

I started to smile and even dance,

while the crowd continued to cheer.

I was filled with joy that I took the chance,

and
that's what
started my

MASCOT CAREER!

Written by Adam Wallace

Cover and internal illustrations by Andy Elkerton

Sourcebooks and the colophon are registered trademarks of Sourcebooks, Inc.

The art was first sketched, then painted digitally with brushes designed by the artist.

Published by Sourcebooks Jabberwocky, an imprint of Sourcebooks, Inc.
P.O. Box 4410, Naperville, Illinois 60563-4410
(630) 961-3900
Fax: (630) 961-2168
sourcebooks.com

Library of Congress Cataloging-in-Publication Data is on file with the publisher.

Source of Production: Shenzhen Wing King Tong Paper Products Co. Ltd., Shenzhen, Longgang District, China
Date of Production: May 2018
Run Number: 5012384

Printed and bound in China.
WKT 10 9 8 7 6 5 4 3 2 1